OUR EIGHT NIGHTS
OF HANUKKAH

by Michael J. Rosen   *illustrated by* DyAnne DiSalvo-Ryan

HOLIDAY HOUSE / New York

The very first night of Hanukkah, we polish the silver menorah that was my great-grandma's. She brought it from Russia maybe a hundred years ago! It's the oldest thing in the house, I think. We all say the prayers together as we light the shammash—that's the tallest candle—and touch it to the first night's candle.

Baby Audrey just burbles, but that kind of sounds like Hebrew. Then we sing Hanukkah songs and take turns reading a story that's even older than Great-grandma's menorah: it's the two-thousand-year-old, true story about this small group of Jews, led by Judah Maccabee, who didn't want to worship statues of cows and give up being Jewish. So they fought against this huge, powerful Syrian army—but, by a real miracle, the Maccabees won. Nobody in *that* story gave Hanukkah presents, especially ones with superheroes or batteries. They were just glad to be free to be Jews.

On the second night, at Grandma and Grampa's, we light two candles with the shammash. Then we take turns grating potatoes so Grandma can fry us all potato pancakes. We always eat too many latkes, and lots of homemade applesauce, too. The latkes are really crispy, kind of like french-fry pancakes, because Grandma fries them in oil.

The oil is supposed to remind us of the lamp that the Maccabees found in the wrecked Temple. It only had about one day's worth of oil in it, but it burned for eight days. This was a sign that God was on their side, and it is why Hanukkah lasts for eight days. Mom says Grandma's latkes last eight days in her stomach, too. You know what's funny? Our dog comes with us to Grandma's, too, and we don't give him latkes, but the next day you can smell the latkes in his fur!

On the third night, the shammash lights three candles, and we search the house for things we want to give away as presents. See, our family has this tradition: before we get any gifts, we gather all the toys and clothes we don't think we'll use next year. We're not rich, but our closets have plenty of clothes and toys—some toys we didn't even have time to play with. So we give these as gifts to people who aren't as lucky as we are, because Mom likes to remind us that Jews believe in tzedakah, which means that even little kids have something extra they can share.

After that, we paint cards and wrapping paper. We decorate them with glitter and snowflakes—but nothing really Jewish or Christian. Who knows what holiday the kids who receive our gifts are going to celebrate? We just write "Happiness" and "Peace," since that's really all we wish.

On the fourth night, with five candles glowing in the window, we wrap our gifts—after we make sure there aren't any loose parts or missing cards or lost men. We erase our smudgy fingerprints and stray crayon marks so everything looks new. Then each gift is wrapped with our homemade paper.

This is also the night our temple has its big Hanukkah party. We bundle up and walk there. The best part is seeing all the lights: menorahs burning in some windows and trees twinkling in others. The lights tell you who's Jewish and who's not, which you don't really know the rest of the year. When I said that to my dad, he said, "Well, Hanukkah's a chance to be proud of your religion."

All the kids from religious school come with their families. We have cookies shaped in the Star of David, and there's cider and coffee, Israeli dancing, and a play about the Maccabees with aluminum foil swords. The preschoolers always dress up as singing dreidels and spin around. I did when I was little, and it made me dizzy.

On the fifth night, we have our big family dinner with Grandma and Grampa and maybe some other relatives. I think all the Jewish holidays are about getting together with your family. Friends from my regular school who don't really know about Hanukkah come, too. On that night, we say the candle-lighting prayers in Hebrew and English.

For dessert Dad gives everyone a net bag with chocolate coins wrapped in gold foil, and then Grampa says he can beat anyone at a game of dreidel. It's not a very hard game; it's just a spinning top with four Hebrew letters: nun, gimmel, hay, and shin, one on each side. The Hebrew letters stand for "Nes Gadol Hayah Sham." Grampa translates it for anyone who can't speak Hebrew (and mine isn't so good). It means "A Great Miracle Happened There"—you know, two thousand years ago. Everybody probably spoke Hebrew really well back then. At the end of the game (which is mostly laughing because we keep eating our winnings) Grampa gives all us kids Hanukkah gelt—real silver dollars—to save for college.

The sixth night, after we light the menorah, we drive our gifts to a shelter. The people there know kids who don't even have houses. Last year, we sent our presents to our neighbor's cousins. They'd lost almost everything in a gigantic flood—even their dog (although they found him, one month later!).

Later, we shop for family presents. Mom and Dad take Baby Audrey, but we older kids go with Grandma and Grampa. They make weird suggestions about what to get our parents, like kitchen towels or trivets. We've already hinted a lot about what *we'd* like, but our parents always surprise us. Grandma and Grampa never try to buy us clothes. We go to giant toy stores to look for things we really need, and Grandma will say, "Well, I don't know, we'll see," but then Grampa says he's going to find the rest room and sneaks back to buy just what we wanted.

Each year on the seventh night, we light our menorah at our very
best of all friends' house. They celebrate Christmas, but they like
Mom's latkes almost as much as I do, so we bring over a giant
platter of them. After dinner they surprise us with Hanukkah
presents, and we help them trim their tree with cranberries and
tinsel and all the ornaments their two cats haven't broken.

When their tree is finished, the room is lit with only our menorah's flames and the strands of Christmas lights. We tuck the presents we bought them under the tree and eat cookies I've sometimes helped decorate earlier in the day. Did I tell you that our Hanukkah is also about people of different religions living alongside one another?

On the last night of Hanukkah, with all nine candles burning, we open our gifts, one at a time so everyone can watch and no one gets cheated out of a thank-you hug. Our dog gets presents, too, even though he isn't Jewish. Half the presents we made ourselves, and the rest we bought with saved-up allowance. Plus, there are packages from relatives who live too far away to come over.

But while we're still sitting on the floor among all the ribbons and boxes, Dad usually says something besides, "Thank-you, everybody." He always says something like, "Aren't we lucky to be able to celebrate our holiday with everyone in our family in this safe place? It's a miracle." Well, now I know he doesn't mean a great miracle, as in the first Hanukkah story. But maybe it's a tiny one. . . . Maybe a lot of tiny miracles add up to a great one if you think about the whole world and all these menorahs glowing in lots and lots of windows, and all that light.

HOW TO SAY THE HEBREW WORDS IN THIS STORY

dreidel (DREY-duhl)

gelt (gelt)

gimmel (GIM-mel)

Hanukkah (han-OOH-kah)

hay (hay)

Judah Maccabee (Joo-dah MA-cah-bee)

latkes (LAT-kehs)

menorah (meh-NOR-ah)

nun (noon)

shammash (SHAY-mehsh)

shin (sheen)

tzedakah (tsah-DAH-kah)

Text copyright © 2000 by Michael J. Rosen
Illustrations copyright © 2000 by DyAnne DiSalvo-Ryan
All Rights Reserved
Printed in the United States of America
First Edition

Library of Congress Cataloging-in-Publication Data
Rosen, Michael J., 1954–
Our eight nights of Hanukkah / by Michael J. Rosen;
illustrated by DyAnne DiSalvo-Ryan.—1st ed.
p. cm.
Summary: A child describes how one family celebrates Hanukkah, including polishing
the silver menorah, lighting the candles, having a special family dinner, and sharing gifts.
ISBN 0-8234-1476-0
1. Hanukkah—Juvenile Literature. [1. Hanukkah. 2. Holidays.]
I. DiSalvo-Ryan, DyAnne, ill. II. Title
BM695.H3 R58 2000   296.4'35—dc21   99-011001